Iris N. Schwartz employs straightforward, clean writing with attitude to tell her stories of family, romance, and coming of age.

— **GAY DEGANI, AUTHOR OF *WHAT CAME BEFORE***

You might be familiar with the characters in this collection. One might be that girl you'd known as a child, another that young woman you'd met on a date. They could be Everyperson; they could be you or me. But the stories go much deeper than that. Iris N. Schwartz uses precise, spiky prose to take us on short journeys across psychic landscapes. We easily experience the sensations and emotions of her characters. And as in many journeys, the destination often is unexpected. It is a place of recognition, yet it can seem foreign. When you get there, you've come to know a little bit more about the people around you — and about yourself.

— **THADDEUS RUTKOWSKI, AUTHOR OF *GUESS AND CHECK***

My Secret Life with
Chris Noth

My Secret Life with Chris Noth

Chris Noth

And Other Stories

Iris N. Schwartz

POETS WEAR PRADA • Hoboken, New Jersey

My Secret Life with Chris Noth

Poets Wear Prada
533 Bloomfield Street, Second Floor
Hoboken, New Jersey 07030
http://pwpbooks.blogspot.com

First North American Publication 2017
First Mass Market Paperback Edition 2017

Grateful acknowledgment is made to the following publications where some of these stories originally appeared:

Bindweed Magazine, *Connotation Press*, *The Flash Fiction Press*, *The Gambler*, *Jellyfish Review*, *Random Sample Review*, *Writing Raw*, and a Rhetaskew publication *Anthology Askew*, Vol. 002 - April 2017: *Love Gone Askew*.

ISBN-13: 978-0-9979811-6-2   ISBN-10: 0-9979811-6-4

Library of Congress Control Number: 2017957444

Printed in the U.S.A.

Front Cover Author Photo: David B. McConeghey

For David B.,
with unbounded love

Table of Contents

These stories are works of fiction.
Any references to real people or real places is used
fictitiously. Other names, characters, places, and events
are products of the author's imagination, and any
resemblance to actual events or places or persons, living
or dead, is entirely coincidental.

My Secret Life with
Chris Noth

GOLDEN OPPORTUNITY
Brooklyn, NY, 1973

I was wearing my bell-bottomed, ass-hugging, rust-colored corduroys when we met. Ribbed turtleneck. He had on a black leather jacket, blue jeans, shirt buttoned low so I could see golden chest hair — and a very large crucifix. We were in a bowling alley. I was there with friends. I don't know who he was with. Probably no one. Who'd want to compete for oxygen with him? Anyway, I wouldn't have noticed another male.

I was 15, had a 17-year-old Jewish boyfriend on his way to chiropractry school. We had parked a lot but hadn't gone all the way. Nor was I planning to.

This bowling alley boy made my whole body hum. I stood there, brazenly eyeing this dark-blond, beatific creature; I didn't hear my friends' voices, didn't smell greasy fries, didn't notice tufts of cigarette smoke. One hundred butterflies opened and closed their wings atop my skin.

How had I existed before this? And could I now doubt the existence of God?

The miracle spoke. "Yes," he laughed, "it's true."

I remained still, hoping he would not comment on the monarchs.

"I saw you staring at my crucifix."

I mumbled something less than erudite, after which he introduced himself as Joey Ortolano.

My mother was going to kill me.

He extended his hand. "A pleasure to meet you, Samantha Gold."

When had I told him my name? The milkweed butterflies continued to beat their wings.

TWO DAYS LATER I was on the phone with him. Away from my mother. In the basement. Oh, I had it *bad* for Joey! The only time I dared enter that hades of water bugs, plumbing back-ups, and mounted deer heads was when I was ordered — by my mother — to hang damp clothes in the backyard. Or to clear out buckets of waste water when the pipes periodically burst.

Now I was in the basement of my own volition, talking to someone I had no business talking to, aware of the nearness of monarchs as I felt the basso of Joey Ortolano caressing me through the telephone.

Could he hear the flapping of butterflies?

"A 17-year-old is too young for you, Samantha. What can he do for you? You need a man."

Joey was 19, a graduate of Kingsborough Community College. The only blond man I had ever seen in person.

I agreed to meet him at the public library three days

later. I knew the location of my library card would be immaterial.

ANDREW, FUTURE CHIROPRACTOR, called me the day before Joey and I were to meet. Andrew must have sensed my distraction. He asked me, twice, if anything was wrong.

I said I was worried about an upcoming Social Studies test.

That was stupid of me. I always received 95 percent or higher on every exam I took in that subject.

I WAS UP half the night imagining outfits for what I couldn't rightfully call a date. The next day I settled on a forest green V-neck sweater. (Andrew had said it brought out my eyes.) Stuffed my curvy self into the rust cords.

What would an Ortolano discuss with a Gold? I'd never spoken to, let alone made surreptitious plans, with any man outside my "tribe." We could discuss Italian Renaissance artists, or, more prosaically, Neapolitan versus Sicilian pizza. I could ask what it was like to attend community college. Was he planning to transfer to a four-year school?

I ARRIVED five minutes past our appointed time. Spotted Joey Ortolano in front of the Travel section. Again I became transfixed by his chest hair and cross. To this day I don't recall one word of our conversation.

———— ⚬⚭⚬ ————

FOUND MYSELF in Joey's place — actually, the ground floor apartment rented out by Joseph Ortolano Sr. and wife. A space so clean and plastic-encased that no water bug would have the cojones to invade. (Maybe my mother should call his to discuss exterminating and housekeeping options. Maybe not.)

I forgot my mother. Forgot Andrew. Forgot the cautions of my friends.

Joey did things to the insides of my elbows, my outer and inner ears, my neck, my eyelids that brought the monarchs back full force. Easily two hundred black-and-orange flying insects!

I felt the blond man's hands against my green V-neck, my rust cords. Heard my heart. Then knocking. Louder. Not my heart. Ringing. *Definitely* not my heart.

MRS. SOMETHING-OR-OTHER, his mother's friend, was looking for Joey's mother. Apparently, Mrs. Ortolano was not upstairs. Did Joey know where she was?

⚬∞⚬

IN THE INTERIM, I'd rushed to the bathroom. Threw water on my cheeks. Straightened my sweater. Realigned my rust cords. Flitting butterflies? Gone.

EARLY NEIL YOUNG

Earlier this year, July 10.

"It buries me to see him that way."

Her psychotherapist, Tom, looked at her intently. "What?"

Karoline Klein collected tissue shreds from her pants. "It hurts me to see him that way."

"You didn't say that." Tom put down his pen. "You said, 'It *buries* me.'"

"Shit." Karoline reached for another tissue then crumbled it unused. "For the last three days, I've had a song in my head that I can't shake."

"Oh?"

She said, almost whispering, "I keep hearing that forlorn harmonica and that sad, high voice."

Tom asked, "Where did you go three days ago?"

———————

FEBRUARY 2. Karoline noticed Jonas immediately: lush, black curls; line-free face; hawkish nose; aggressively angular jaw. She watched him tear open three sugar packets then rush the contents into his coffee with the stem-end of a plastic spoon.

Karoline averted her eyes, but he had caught her — imagining him forking one of his two coffee cake rectangles then feeding it to her, slowly. She pictured him wiping errant crumbs from her chin and dotting them on his own tongue.

He smiled. Karoline blushed.

Jonas introduced himself. He didn't offer cake.

———

JULY 7. She recalled what her therapist, Tom, had said about dating. "You can discover everything you need to know about someone in the first five minutes after you've met."

In February, Karoline had observed that Jonas was an enthusiastic consumer of coffee and sweets.

Now, she watched Jonas in his bed. He slowly moved his right hand toward the call button. Karoline blinked several times to clear her vision then walked into his room. She held a bouquet in front of her.

Jonas opened his mouth. No sound. He tried to reach his unresponsive right leg with his right arm, couldn't, looked away. With his left hand, Jonas pulled his hospital gown tighter around his midsection. Miniature gray bears danced across his stomach.

Karoline put out a hand; it stayed, motionless, in the air for several seconds. She should have brought a pad and pen.

A nurse walked in. *Thank God*, thought Karoline.

"What beautiful flowers! Aren't those beautiful, Mr. Mendel? I'll get someone to put them in a vase." The nurse walked away.

Come back, thought Karoline. *Come back!*

Karoline refilled his plastic water pitcher. Walked the halls on a quest for a pad as well as hermetically sealed apple slices. And searched for Jonas's doctors to determine the extent of her boyfriend's right-side weakness, aphasia, and balance issues.

She succeeded in keeping him hydrated — and questionably nourished with browning Macintosh slices — but found just one nurse and left messages for three doctors. Once back in his room, she realized she'd forgotten to look for a pad and pen.

Jonas was weeping. Where was the rectangular cardboard tissue box she'd seen earlier next to his right foot? Karoline didn't know what to do. She was afraid to touch him, afraid she would "catch" his stroke.

∽

TWO MINUTES LATER, Karoline was sitting on the toilet in Jonas's bathroom, chanting the refrain of that song that would continue to haunt her with its persistent, anguished tune.

She looked down to find the tissue box in her left hand. How long had she been holding it?

ᴄᴏ

ON HER WAY HOME from the hospital, Karoline recalled Jonas tossing boxes of coffee cake and doughnuts into their cart every time they went shopping. She would return the boxes, fill plastic bags with apples: Jonagolds, Ida Reds, Honeycrisps. Karoline promised Jonas these treats were naturally sweet. He'd laugh and never eat them, buy cake when she wasn't around.

———

JULY 8. Now his black curls were tinged with gray. The 38-inch-waist pants Jonas wore when they met no longer zipped. His skin was flaky and itchy, probably due to diabetes. She would bring Jonas new pants — and aloe vera gel. *Didn't the hospital have lotion?*

———

JULY 9. In the morning Karoline dreamed she and Jonas held hands in a double coffin. Both wore gold wedding bands. The coffin was being lowered into the ground at Mount Hebron Cemetery in Queens, New York — one plot away from her parents' graves. The casket was open. Karoline batted away soil. Jonas could not move his arms, so dirt filled up his side of the casket.

Six feet from the shared grave site, The Band and Neil Young performed an especially raw rendition of "Helpless." Large numbers of Kleins and Mendels were keening.

UNSUNG

New York, 1970

A t home, Candy sat like a dog and tried to speak only when spoken to. That is, she sat in a chair and tried not to wiggle or talk. Ma said her daughter was noisy. She said Candy's singing echoed like thunder, pitched her a migraine.

Candy used to belt like Janis Joplin and Ethel Merman. Once she presented "An Evening of Janis and La Merm" to an audience composed of her father, mother, brother, her brother's friend Elliot — who happened to stop by — and two goldfish. Every audience member was appreciated.

Now she sat on a kitchen chair and read a Social Studies chapter on The Great Depression while slathering slice after slice of Pepperidge Farm white bread with Philadelphia cream cheese. When Candy finished a page, she'd spread the soft cheese on a slice, fold the bread horizontally so the ends would meet, trim the crusts, eat them, smash the bread until it was crepe thin, then methodically chew and swallow her concoction.

Depending on the length of a chapter — for any class — Candy might polish off one-half to three-quarters of a loaf in one sitting. She only did this when Ma was out of the house. Let Ma think Candy's brother Leonard, and maybe Elliot, downed a king's serving of bread and cream cheese.

Everything irked Ma now that Dad was dead. The way Ma cried, wore coffee-stained housedresses, and never talked except to order Candy and Leonard around, you'd believe Ma was the only one affected.

And now Candy couldn't sing in the house. No more ecstatic performances, long hair flying, eyes squeezed shut. No roaring of Broadway favorites, no holding of notes forever. So, she read. Not just school books. Louisa May Alcott, Joseph Heller, J.D. Salinger, James Baldwin, Eudora Welty, Henry Miller, *The New York Times*, *The World Book Encyclopedia* (all volumes), *The Oxford English Dictionary* (alas, abridged). Whatever reading material Candy found, she devoured.

Candy often dreamed that Dad was alive. He'd sit by her bed and invite her to a Hitchcock film festival, whisper in her ear that just the two of them would go; Ma and Leonard would have to stay home. His deep, quiet voice would morph into something shrill and bellowing, and to her great distaste Candy would be staring into Ma's face.

"Wake up, there's no time to dilly-dally; who do you think you are to sleep late?"

Candy wasn't religious, but she prayed hard that Dad would visit her the next night. They could perform duets.

WATERING HOLE

On their first date, Marcus met Naomi with spindly purple flowers. He called her "zaftig in a very appealing way."

What was left of his hair was chestnut brown. His eyes were lake blue, his cheeks pink.

By way of explaining his faux pas, Marcus said, "They tell me at my favorite watering hole that I can be a jackass. I mean, sometimes, I offer opinions before being fully informed."

Naomi said, "You mean, sometimes, you're a jackass?"

She told him she was kidding, and Marcus took her hand as she reached for her water.

Naomi felt a shock as their fingers touched, and she audibly gasped.

HE PUT UP bookshelves for her and a small, free-standing CD tower. He grappled with screwdrivers and nails, sweated. Naomi felt a jolt in her nether region as she watched Marcus *shirtless* work with tools and wood. Somehow she managed to keep from kissing his naked head until he finished.

———— ∞∞ ————

Marcus hung his head sheepishly as he told her of getting drunk — after work — at his favorite watering hole. He'd ordered a round for his friends, then another. He'd spent too much money that night and didn't have a credit card with him, so he couldn't take a taxi home.

At three in the morning on a Tuesday, Marcus, jelly legged, walked the streets of downtown Brooklyn. He said he must have made an irresistible target. Two men told him to give them his wallet. He hesitated, tried to explain he had little money. One of the muggers grabbed Marcus's wallet, took the remaining five-dollar bill, and tossed the wallet to the ground. He stomped on it, screamed at Marcus. Man number two asked Marcus to give them his ring and watch.

"They were gifts, Naomi, from my grandfather," Marcus confided. "I tried to reason with them."

This was why, when she met him at the movie theater on Saturday night, his right eyelid and surrounding tissue were varying shades of mauve and yellow. This is why he held his side when he laughed during the film.

———— ∞∞ ————

"WHY DO YOU want to go out with me?" Marcus asked her more than once.

Couldn't he see what she saw? An intelligent, articulate, generous man, sexy, humble as hell.

———— ∞∞ ————

WHEN NAOMI STAYED over at his tastefully furnished apartment, he didn't offer her coffee or dessert. They had already eaten dinner, so she chalked it up to that. Or to the immense bulge in his pants that she felt when he kissed her.

The next morning, as Marcus snored quietly, Naomi put on his shirt and walked to the kitchen. She would surprise him with breakfast. Maybe challah French toast, strawberries, coffee. She opened the refrigerator door onto two bottles of Pinot Grigio. On the tiled floor, to the right of the fridge, was a carton of wine bottles. She opened two kitchen cabinets: no canned tuna, no soup, no dishes. Nothing.

Naomi returned to the bedroom, kissed him on his bald head, and retreated into the bathroom to shower and dress.

She was shaking as she closed the apartment door behind her.

SENSE

E very day I awaken to soft masses of color. Innocent mahogany, burgundy, plum, white. Lights brighten, shadows deepen. In the evening, bulbs and lampshades radiate, appear haloed. Tiny green lights on my router are suffused and barely visible until I am inches in front of it.

This is because I am deeply myopic and astigmatic. Before I put my eyeglasses on in the morning, the mahogany dressers, burgundy bedroom curtains, plum bedsheets and pillowcases, and Navajo White walls are hued clouds cushioning my way into the world. The longer I leave off my glasses or don't insert contact lenses, the less threatening my surroundings.

I wish I could go about my life minus eye gear, but, as I am legally blind, vehicles are colored blurs, too, and in scant minutes I'd cross a thoroughfare and get run over. Growing pools of deep, objectively attractive red would accompany my own pale vagueness, but it would hurt me as much as it would any seeing person.

So I don corrective lenses, grudgingly, right after I rise from my bed.

Some days I yearn to be deaf. To be able to wake up to a quiet Manhattan: no drilling concrete, no neighbors' techno music, no blaring TVs! Even pigeons cooing becomes banal if you hear them enough.

What a blessing it would be if I lost my olfactory glands. Burnt toast aroma assaulting the nose in the a.m.? Gone. Greasy chicken and stinky cabbage emanating from Apartment 8R? History. Gas leaks? I'll never know. If I die, I die. I can think of worse ways to go.

Some mornings I dimly remember a woman's face looking intently at mine from outside the bars of a crib. Or was that metal of a cage? Both? And what of the man's face with blurry stubble?

THE LIGHT SHOW

W hen Jessie Jean finally remembered the name, she smiled so widely that her grin sounded like it was cracking her face. She impulsively tried to clap her hands with joy, but of course the ten-year-old could not wrest free of the torn bedsheets that tied her arms (and legs) to the patio chair.

Jessie Jean's mind had wandered again. She possessed an inclination to follow her wandering mind with her body, and so, according to Bobby Earl, she caused this mess. The girl, however, figured this unpleasantness existed on account of the two of them being too much for Mom-Mom and Pop-Pop — even though they cared for her and her brother only on weekends.

Thirteen-year-old Bobby Earl had confided in his sister, during a stolen moment outside their respective closets, that "The Light Show" gave him relief.

From her brother's closet at the opposite end of the ranch house, he communicated with Jessie Jean — don't ask her how — the power of the show. Used to be they needed their hands free, balled up into fists, to rub hard on the outside of their eyelids. Rubbing, the boy promised, produced sky-blue, fuchsia, orange, pineapple-yellow, and, best of all, purple lightning-like flashes, against the dead black inside their eyelids. This, he intoned — like a zealous preacher — yielded variety, beauty, and, especially, freedom from the blackness. The Light Show would save them.

Once Jessie Jean perfected her know-how outside the closet, she could manufacture the show inside — without the use of hands.

The Light Show bestowed more than brightness. The ten-year-old discovered this on her own last Saturday afternoon. At the spirit, the spark — no, the spur of the moment — she'd call out to her colors, her blessed lights.

Fuchsia lightning became her friend, Bailey Anne; orange, Jayson Joe; pineapple yellow, Shakirah Leigh. And so on, for as many hues as Jessie Jean could imagine. These flashes paradoxically stayed with her and thus freed her — from darkness — and from bedeviling loneliness and fear.

Between the infrequent meal and toilet breaks, the long stretches without either grandparent or brother, Jessie Jean felt touched by the love of her colorful friends. She did not, however, share her discovery with Bobby Earl. He needed to find out on his own. She tempted shame by keeping these new friends for herself; the girl wasn't sure she could bear it if they left her for her brother.

And so, the girl never told her brother of her deepened relationship with The Light Show. Even on Sunday nights — when Mama fetched the siblings to take them home for the coming school week — even then, she did not tell him.

Last Sunday, when he spotted red indentations on his sister's right wrist and begged her not to complain to Mom-Mom or Pop-Pop, she agreed — and, yes, she wouldn't inform Mama. But she wouldn't tell her brother how to make friends with The Light Show either. And this time, she decided, would be *the last time* she'd give in.

When her grandmother, shortly after, told Jessie Jean, once again, that keeping her and Bobby Earl in the dark made them appreciate the light, that being immobilized helped them understand freedom, it was with the strength of friends like Shakirah Leigh that the ten-year-old was able to hold her tongue.

A COUPLE

R onny remembered with an ache in his gut the days and nights before Sophie.

He had had no one to cuddle with, no one to wrap his arms around in his toasty bed while whispering his woes into a willing ear. Ronny was reticent with his colleagues and friends but nonetheless needed someone who'd accept his abundance of affection.

He yearned for another homebody to share his succulent specialties: T-bone steak with balsamic vinegar reduction, cremini mushrooms, and smashed sweet potatoes; cream-added scrambled eggs, with ultra-crisp bacon and oversized biscuits.

So what if these weren't the healthiest meals? If you didn't celebrate life, what was the point?

He wanted someone to run with in the park, someone who could keep up, and maybe surpass him in a 10-K race. Someone to look back as she gained the advantage, urge him on.

Ronny would never forget the day they met: Her warm brown eyes fixed on him; her full body accepted his eager arms.

Seven years together; then, without complaint or portent, one day Sophie was someone else. Confused, stumbling, unable to communicate.

He called friends, family for support, knowing with bitterness that the one who'd always lent the most support was now the one who couldn't offer it.

Many doctors, little hope.

Sophie worsened, quicker than he could accept. Her brown eyes lost their luster. She refused even Ronny's best culinary efforts.

In the end, all he could do was whisper his love for her, caress her neck and back.

After a decent interval, still knowing he might never find anyone who compared, Ronny donned running shorts and T-shirt, laced his shoes, and made his way to Sophie's last doctor.

He thought he might find another set of brown eyes to gaze at him as Sophie's had, and so Ronny pulled her leash from his shorts pocket and rang the bell on the vet's door.

Ronny was no good alone.

SO SAID LYNETTE

When she was five years old, Lynette began rewriting her life as a novel. (She was three when she started reading.) Now she is nine.

Lynette's real-life parents, Bill and Sarah Smythe, put back vermouth and inhaled Marlboros. Bill, six feet four inches, possessed the frame of a man who eats only when prodded. Sarah, thin but shapely from afar, up close exhibited a fine network of facial wrinkles often bestowed upon the nicotine-addicted. Lynette's friends thought Mr. and Mrs. Smythe exotic, envied Lynette her flaccid parental bonds.

Lynette never told her friends that, most weekend mornings, she vacuumed heaping ashtrays and washed sour-smelling highball glasses; and then prepared pancakes, sausages, and fresh-squeezed orange juice for herself and older brother Jimmy. She washed and dried breakfast pans and dishes. Checked on her parents, always finding them, fully clothed and snoring, on their extra-long bed. This was comforting as well as worrisome for nine-year-old Lynette.

John and Judy Wilson, the parents in her book, drank

only cold water or tea, and toked Jamaican weed solely on special occasions. They didn't throw parties for adults; they planned fun and educational family events.

Lynette's alter ego, Kendra, an average-height brunette with above-average looks, had no trouble making friends, and was expert at double-Dutch jump rope and online games.

In her novel, Jimmy did not exist. Rather, Lynette replaced him with a Dalmatian dog, Tintype. Was Tintype a silly, quaint name? In her book, "So Said the Wilsons," no name was silly.

Lynette kept the novel a secret. Once in a while, when Bill or Sarah tried to shake free of an alcoholic haze, one or the other would ask why Lynette took her "little briefcase" into the bathroom. They didn't wait for an answer, just mentioned it to their boozehound friends as if it were the cutest thing in the world.

The girl disdained the lot of them.

In the bathroom Lynette could think. Cry. Write. Breathe. Some days she felt lucky no one in the family suffered digestive problems, especially when she locked herself in for an hour at a time.

She wanted to make the Smythes suffer. Bender Bill micturated in his pants in front of his daughter. Sloshed Sarah exhaled smoke rings into Lynette's face. Jism Jimmy addressed Lynette as "Skelet-O" or "Miss Ugh." For all that and more, she wished them ill. Or dead. It didn't make her proud of herself. It gave her relief.

———— ✐ ————

PARAGRAPH ONE from "So Said the Wilsons":

> Every year John and Judy Wilson planned intricate escapades for their only child, Kendra, to bolster her intellectual, social, and physical well-being. This Saturday was "Excavate Your Treasure Day," complete with crayon-wrought treasure maps, hand-sewn pirate costumes, and Judy's special combination pink lemonade & honeyed green tea. John had been planting "little boxes of fun" for a week, on the grounds and inside their two-story home. Both parents worked hard to provide Kendra — and pet Dalmatian Tintype — a *bootiful* time!

———— ✐ ————

HER OPENING PARAGRAPH makes Lynette want to retch. She will improve it as she's a fearsome editor. Plus, writing the book transports her to another zone: a caring-parent, loyal-dog zone, free of self-abusing brothers, where every living creature is hers to mastermind.

She's sure "So Said the Wilsons" will sell. Longer term, the kiddie novel should allow Lynette Smythe to emancipate herself. To leave this booze-soaked dunghill and its denizens behind.

That Saturday, the Smythe parents were throwing one of their disgusting soirees, which meant Jimmy would have to go to the basement, or a friend's house, or under a rock, or behind a giant trash cart to compulsively masturbate.

Lynette would have to stay in her room most of the night or ride miles away with her laptop on her unicorn Destiny.

Oh, for a day with John and Judy Wilson! An afternoon whispering to Tintype and brushing his coat! Lynette would swear off *Candy Crush.* Quit jumping rope. Even lock away her laptop — no access to "So Said the Wilsons"! No texting friends! — for a month.

ON SUNDAY MORNING, Jimmy was not in his room. His bedcovers were not in their usual disarray. Backpack and cell phone were gone. No stench of sweat. No cum-stained socks. Lynette felt flutters of panic in her stomach and throat.

She ran to her parents' bedroom to alert them. No Bill! No Sarah! Only a wrinkled bedspread. No keys on the dresser; no wallet, no purse!

Lynette covered her mouth with her hand to slow her breathing. She sat on the rug in the living room and shook back and forth. The nine-year-old envisioned Bill and Sarah, bloody, under a truck; Jimmy, mangled, inside a dumpster, face half-hidden by fast food wrappers and paper coffee cups.

For the first time that morning, Lynette noticed the living room was devoid of overflowing ashtrays, dirty glasses, and soiled cocktail napkins. No cigarette smell, either. She peered through the windows overlooking the Smythe driveway: No SUV. *What was going on here?*

How would Lynette be able to continue her schooling? What would happen when she ran out of food? Who would pay the mortgage? How would she celebrate her tenth birthday tomorrow?

As unlikely as it seemed, Lynette knew that had to be it. Her parents and brother must have left early — and stealthily — to buy her a birthday gift! Sarah and Bill must have cleaned up all party detritus last night before collapsing into bed and conspired, along with Jimmy, to make Lynette the happiest ten-year-old in the neighborhood.

Lynette could barely believe her luck. Could Bill and Sarah Smythe live up to John and Judy Wilson? The nearly-ten-year-old felt tired from sudden excitement and good fortune. It was, after all, early Sunday morning. She hadn't slept enough — or eaten. Now was a perfect time to sit on the couch and wait for her family. Surely they would bring breakfast back.

WARM. WARM ... AND SOFT. Movement. Licking. Lynette raised her head. Dalmatian puppy breath warmed her cheeks. This adorable creature was running around her, then to her, panting in her face and licking her cheeks.

"Finally!" Judy took a drink of cold water, laughed, then called to her husband, who was rolling a diminutive joint in the kitchen. "John, Kendra's back! Bring that weed in here."

Judy turned back to her daughter. "I think Tintype was scared he'd never play with you again! Be a dear and bring us some rolling papers now, would you?"

MY SECRET LIFE WITH CHRIS NOTH

I 'm five feet, blond, supercurvaceous. An unknown writer living in Washington Heights. Pretty! He's a tall man, a manly man. A famous actor with a beauteous beak of a nose, Dick Tracy jawline, thick head of hair in need of my talented fingers. He's Chris Noth, star of TV programs that repeat and repeat until I can't get Noth out of my head. My heart. Other parts I'm too classy to mention.

Chris dated models. I'm no model. I couldn't grow taller, but I could lose weight. And I did. Lose weight.

Then I wrote an in-depth analysis of his major TV roles, from Detective Mike Logan on *Law & Order* to Mr. Big on *Sex and the City*, to Detective Mike Logan on *Law & Order: Criminal Intent*, to Peter Florrick on *The Good Wife*. I wrote it on spec for *TV Guide.* They grabbed it, because, through deep personal connections I didn't have until I forged them in my imagination, I snared an interview with Chris.

Mr. Gorgeous and I produced sparkling conversation for hours, even after the interview had been completed. He'd been kind enough to meet me in my "upstate" Manhattan neighborhood, at La Reina del Bistec on upper Broadway. As he also has an abiding fondness for *plátanos maduros* (he confided during our first meeting), I knew I would see him again.

Chris was unable to get together that second time but left a coy note with the manager of La Cabaña Dominicana, where we were to enjoy our "follow-up interview."

He had not forgotten me.

Over the next few weeks, he left little post-its for me at various Dominican restaurants in the Heights. Chris never told me where I could find them, but I always did.

One night, Chris visited me during REM stage. I know he had eighteen trysts with a prostitute — no, Peter Florrick did that — but still, he gives me shivers. He is imposing and charismatic. Somehow, by the end of one dream, not only had we exchanged sly looks, but I ended up wearing his briefs, Chris Noth-redolent and warm. When I woke up I felt dirty, excited, and guilty. What more could a woman want? I appreciated the attention, as well as his low-tech methods of communication. Yet, like Mr. Big, he was noncommittal.

Detective Sexy continued to pop up in my dreams.

Early one Sunday, I opened my eyes to the horrific truth— fueled by an IMDb update — that Chris Noth is married and, in fact, a father!

Thank God. Or the Heavens. Or whoever writes Internet Movie Database. Because I have *my own man*. I love him. I do. And, frankly, I wasn't looking forward to leaving him for a guy like Peter Florrick or Mr. Big, or even Detective Mike

Logan. Plus, it's been murder trying to lose these last ten pounds.

Acknowledgments

My thanks to the publishers and editors of the various publications where some of these works originally appeared, sometimes in a slightly different format or version:

Anthology Askew, Vol. 002 - April 2017: *Love Gone Askew*, a Rhetaskew publication	"A Couple"
Bindweed Magazine	"So Said Lynette"
Connotation Press	"The Light Show" (under the title "Light") and "Sense"
The Flash Fiction Press	"Golden Opportunity"
The Gambler	"Unsung"
Jellyfish Review	"My Secret Life with Chris Noth" (as "Nothern Manhattan: My Secret Life with Chris Noth")
Random Sample Review	"Early Neil Young"
Writing Raw	"Watering Hole"

Special thanks to Madeline Artenberg, Marilyn Jaye Lewis, and Brenda Morisse, each of whom read various drafts of these stories, for their honesty, patience, and invaluable suggestions.

With much appreciation to Lydia B. Schwartz and Digby Beaumont for consistent encouragement and enthusiasm for my fiction writing, before and during the making of this book.

Special gratitude to David B. McConeghey, whose ear and eye for details enabled me to form more vivid characters.

About the Author

Iris N. Schwartz is the author of more than forty works of fiction. She is currently working on a novel comprised of flash chapters. Her literary fiction has been published in dozens of journals and anthologies, including *101 Words*, *Flash Fiction Friday*, *Gravel*, and *Quail Bell Review*. In addition, Ms. Schwartz has written erotica, most notably the story "Hedonics," anthologized in *Stirring Up a Storm: Tales of the Sensual, the Sexual, and the Erotic* (Running Press). *Awakened*, a collection of her poems with those of Madeline Artenberg, was published by Rogue Scholars Press. *My Secret Life with Chris Noth: And Other Stories* is her first short short story collection. Ms. Schwartz lives in New York City with actor David B. McConeghey.

ABOUT THE TYPE

Text for this book is set in Bookman Old Style, designed by Ong Chong Wah (b. 1955) for Monotype and released in 1990. The Malaysian-born graphic and font designer studied and worked in England, mostly in advertising prior to Monotype. His credits also include the ever-popular Footlight (Monotype) and Ocean Sans (Adobe) among a total of nine type families.

Ong's Bookman Old Style is characterized by the near-vertical stress of its face, heavy type color, wide letters, and the somewhat taller lowercase characteristic of hymn and classic children's books. Ong based his digitized design on various 1960s and 1970s phototypesetting revivals of Alexander Phemister's classic Old Style Antique (circa 1858) cut for the Miller and Richard foundry in Edinburgh, Scotland as a "modern" recasting of the Caslon typeface cut by William Caslon in the 1720s.

Despite its "old style" moniker and look — or perhaps because of it — Ong's design continues to prevail. Title designer Victoria Vaus selected Bookman Old Style for the main title of the 1999 film *Election*, a high school comedy starring Matthew Broderick and Reese Witherspoon, directed by Alexander Payne. Later the typeface was adopted for the original Tumblr logo (2007–2013) by designer Peter Vidani — prior to Yahoo! acquisition mid-2013. Bookman Old Style was chosen here for its legibility, classic storybook styling, and general good humor.